Hannah and her Gra

By Deborah A. Woodthorpe

Illustrated by Kulthum Burgess

We were walking on the fell, just my Grandma and I, when I asked her a question that had been bothering me for a long time. 'Grandma,' I said, 'why don't you believe in Allah like we do – Mummy, Daddy, Mustafa and me?' Grandma wasn't a Muslim. Mummy had changed her religion to Islam when she was young and still at school, before she even met my father. Grandma and Granddad were unsure of what they believed. They sometimes said they were 'Christians'. They didn't go to Church, though, and they didn't believe in the Bible much, either. Grandma said that she was 'agnostic'. That means she thinks we can never know for sure if there is a God or not.

'Why did you ask that?' she said very stiffly. 'What does it matter what I believe?'

'I am just curious,' I said. 'I want to understand why you don't pray five times a day like us, or fast in Ramadan, or give regular charity, or want to visit the Ka'bah in Makkah. I want to understand why you don't believe in God.' We continued to walk up the fell. Grandma was silent, deep in thought as she frowned and pulled her lips into a tight line. 'Well,' she finally said as we neared the gate at the end of the first field, 'I just don't think there is enough proof that God exists. And even if there *was* a God,' she continued, 'why would He want us to worship Him all the time anyway? Why would He want us to live in fear of Him?'

Now it was my turn to screw up my face as I thought about what Grandma had just said. We continued to make our way over a

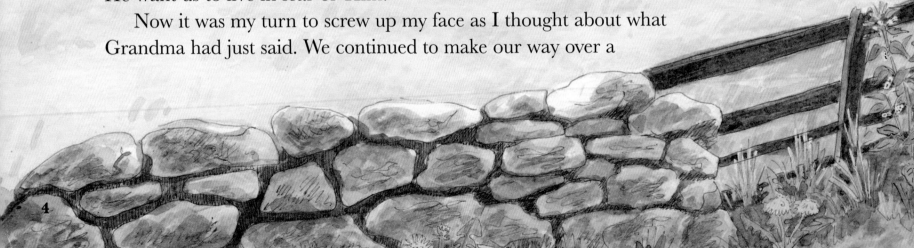

wooden stile, then over a little bridge that crossed a stream, through another gate and into the next, larger field where no crops were being grown because it was being left fallow to rest the soil. The beauty of the field made us both stop suddenly and look. There in front of us were the most beautiful wild flowers – all in full, glorious colour, all fragrant and full of life. There was also a hum of excitement in the air – dragonflies, bees, butterflies, birds all carried on their work and play as if we were invisible to them, and we watched, silently, their happy dance. *'Subhan-Allah,'* I said. *'Masha'Allah.* How beautiful!'

'It *is* beautiful here on these fells,' she said as though she was really talking to herself. Then she shook herself slightly and said, 'Come on! We can't stand here all day. Let's get to the top of the fell.' And off she set, steaming on ahead up the little mud footpath to the gate in the distance.

I like walking with my Grandma. She always sees the fun in everything. Often we don't even finish our walks to the top of the fell because we've spent so long counting beetles, or birds, or frogspawn that it's almost dark and time for the evening prayer when we've finished and we have to go home instead. But today we don't play in the mud by the stream, or look under old logs or rocks. Today Grandma is thinking and I run after her trying to keep up. 'Grandma', I said, out of breath, 'I think there is proof that God exists – lots and lots of proof. And', I continued, 'I don't think He wants us to live in fear of Him. I think… I think that when we worship we are just telling the truth…'

'What do you mean?' said Grandma with her forehead furrowed again. 'Worship isn't about telling the truth. It's about praying and kneeling and all that.'

'Well,' I closed my eyes to think of a way to get my thoughts into words, 'when I worship or pray, I feel like I am writing a thank you note to God. Like when you bought me my bike at Eid… I didn't go and thank someone else for it, did I?'

'Well, why would you?' retorted Grandma. '*I* bought it for you. Why would you thank someone else?'

'That's what I mean, Grandma. When I pray, I always remember where everything came from, and where I'm going – because I'm not going to live forever – I'm travelling back to God. And when I pray I remember that God is the Owner of everything and I'm just telling the truth by saying that.'

We reached the next gate, which was surrounded by thicket and hedgerow, and just as I finished climbing the stile, I spotted something glinting in the sun under a big oak tree.

'What's that?' I asked excitedly. 'What?' said Grandma,

as though I had woken her from a sleep. 'That! That glinting thing under the tree! Come on, Grandma – I'll race you!' and with that I ran towards the big oak tree. Grandma didn't run. Grandma often strides but never runs, and even if she did she would probably always let me win anyway. I got to the tree, and what do you think I found under that old oak tree in the third field on the fell above my Grandma's town? You would never guess in a million years! You would never guess because it was a one-in-a-million find!

Grandma caught up to me and stood looking at what I was staring at. 'It's a ring,' she said plainly. Then looking closer and leaning over the bush under the oak tree, which had somehow entangled the ring, she said, 'It's an old ring.' She managed to retrieve the ring by breaking some of the branches (and I said *Astaghfirullah* under

my breath for breaking the bush like that). 'Goodness me! This is a *very* old ring!

Very old *indeed*. How marvellous, Hannah! You've found a Roman artefact! A Roman ring!'

'How do you know that, Grandma?' I asked wondering if I would be allowed to keep it.

'Well, do you remember that archaeological dig I went on a few years back – you know, the one with the TV people here who were filming that history programme? Do you remember we were looking for things that showed how people lived a long time ago? Well, we unearthed a ring just like this. It was Roman.'

'What would a Roman ring be doing all the way out here in this field?' I said, looking around me.

'The Romans used to rule Britain, Hannah. This town, even though it is small today, was once a very important centre in Roman times. There was a fort about three miles away, and the town surrounding it was a good-sized market place for traders, travellers on their way to Scotland and the Borders, and for the Roman soldiers posted here. In the olden days there were no such things as banks to keep your money and jewellery safe in, so people used to bury their treasure to keep it safe from robbers. They would plant it near a landmark so that when they came to dig it up, perhaps years later, they could remember where they buried it. And this tree is very old, but do you suppose it is as old as the Romans?' she asked herself more than me. 'Maybe another tree stood here – the grandmother of this tree…'

I was thinking about what Grandma had told me – about the treasure under the tree and who might have put it there, and how much it was worth when Grandma said while looking at the ring, 'Just think of the person who made this! I wonder who made it. I wonder who bought it. I wonder who buried it and why – and why they never returned for it. I wonder what happened to them. Maybe it was a wedding ring…' She went on and on. I had never seen my Grandma so excited about anything in my whole life before! She was like a little girl. Her eyes had a sparkle that you don't often find in grown-ups.

'Maybe,' I said, 'there's other treasure buried under there as well, then.'

'Yes,' said Grandma with several sturdy nods of her head, 'you could be right. There may be other artefacts hidden here. We must remember exactly where the ring was found when we inform the authorities when we hand it in…'

'What do you mean? Aren't we keeping it?' I asked, dismayed.

'We can't − it might be important and something that the nation should own. You know, it might be best kept in a museum so everyone can see it. Maybe they'll want to come and dig here to see what else they can find…'

'But *I* found it!' I moaned.

'Let's find out for sure first.' With that she took a handkerchief out of her pocket, unfolded it, placed the ring inside, carefully wrapped it up and put the package into her jacket pocket.

We stood for a while longer looking at the bush we had found the ring ensnared in. 'It must have been pushed up when the bush grew through the earth catching the ring at the same time. How amazing! What are the chances of that happening? A Roman ring lying hidden for thousands of years and then a bush growing around it in just the right way to push it into the open… and then we come along and find it! What a find!' Then she put her hands into her pockets and with a fresh spring in her step said, 'C'mon,' and continued up the fell on the old footpath.

Grandma chatted about the ring, the Romans, the archaeological dig she had been on – about lots of things, and I thought about the conversation we were having before all the excitement and about how my Grandma was not a Muslim. It made me sad again. 'Grandma,' I said, putting my arm through hers, 'why don't you just learn about Islam a little bit. Why don't you read the Qur'an and find out about…?'

Grandma turned to me sharply, pulled her arm away and said, 'Why do you keep going on and on about God and religion all the time? Why can't you just let people live their lives the way they want? I don't want to read the Qur'an. I don't want to know about God – Allah – or whatever you call Him. I don't want to know about the Prophets and I don't want to pray all the time either! For goodness sake, Hannah, let's just live and let live, shall we?'

I was hurt and shocked by Grandma's anger. I had never seen my Grandma angry before. I went quiet and almost cried, but instead I pursed my lips together and swallowed hard. I couldn't talk, because if I had tried I would have cried. All I could do was whisper in a hoarse voice, 'But I love you, Grandma, and I want us to live together forever in Heaven.'

Maybe it was the cold air that had sprung up over the fell top, but suddenly I felt very cold and did not really feel like walking or talking anymore. We were nearing the fell top when Grandma stooped down to pick something up. 'Oh dear,' she said. 'Somebody has lost their watch. Look, Hannah, that's two things we've found today.'

I looked and saw in my grandmother's hand an old, shiny, analogue watch. It didn't look very valuable to me, or very interesting either. I was still hurt and instead of admiring our new find I scuffed the toe of my shoe, kicking the mud off and staring at it intently. Grandma was rattling on and on about our good luck at finding two things today and how marvellous the watch was, how well made it was, how beautiful the craftsmanship, when all of a sudden I had an idea! A *brilliant* idea!

'Grandma,' I said brightly, 'I don't believe in Romans.'

'What?' she said, looking very confused as she glanced up from the watch.

'I don't believe in Romans,' I said, clearing my throat.

'Well, it doesn't matter if you *believe* in them or not – they existed. They formed a very important part of world history, whether you like it or not.'

'No,' I said quietly. 'I don't believe they were here at all. I think some men probably invented the stories about the Romans to try to make sense of our history and where we came from.'

'You what?' my Grandma said. 'That's the daftest thing I ever heard! Of course they existed! Where do you think we get all our artefacts from? What about all the evidence we have?'

'I don't call that evidence,' I said. 'I think that all the artefacts just appeared in the ground one day. There's no proof that anyone put them there. They just happened to form in the ground like that. And,' I continued authoritatively, 'I don't believe that watch belongs to anyone and it doesn't have a maker. It appeared on the ground like that in one piece – by accident. All the pieces fell into place by coincidence.'

I looked at my Grandma to see if my plan was working. She was looking at me as though she was trying to unravel a piece of string with her eyes – mouth agape and nose screwed up a little. 'What's got into you? How can a watch just fall together by accident? That's impossible.'

'Why is it impossible?' I protested.

'Because… because… well, because watches are *made*, that's why. They are made of metal, they don't just grow on trees!'

'But Roman artefacts do – we saw that ring growing on the tree with our own eyes!'

'Hannah, watches have cogs. People make cogs. People have to put the cogs in the right order otherwise the watch wouldn't work. If you look at a watch you can see a design and that means someone designed it. Designs don't happen by accident. Cogs don't fall into place in just the right order by accident. The same with archaeology and history; the artefacts didn't grow in the ground, people put them there. These things are too complex to happen by accident!'

I walked past my Grandma to the rocky tip of the fell that overlooked the valley below, a main road, and a river. 'And cars, and computers? Were they made?'

'Yes.'

'And TVs and aeroplanes?'

'Yes, *all* of them were designed and made.'

'They didn't just happen by accident?'

'No, dear, all of them were built with a purpose.'

23

I looked at my Grandma, wondering when she would understand what she had just admitted without realising it. 'Well, what about the universe, then?'

'What?' she said stiffly. 'Grandma, look, we got excited because we found a ring someone buried thousands of years ago, and a watch someone lost and we see how beautifully made they are. But when I say I think they got here by accident, you say they have marvellous craftsmanship and they must have been designed, and only people can design things. But I think the world and the universe are more beautiful and more complex than a ring and an old watch. I don't think the world and the universe could have got here by accident either. So who made all this?' and I swung my arms open in a semi-circle all around me. 'Who made the planet that we walk on and the air that we breathe? Who gave us eyes and a beating heart? Who made us clever enough to make the ring and build the watch? Who gave us intelligence? Who gave us everything that we take for granted, Grandma?'

Grandma looked at me very thoughtfully and then gazed down at the valley behind and below me, and then at the watch in her hand. She didn't say anything.

'Grandma, I don't feel like all this could be an accident for no reason. And isn't it right for us to thank the One who gave us this? My Mum says we have to thank a stranger for holding a door open for us, so I think I have to thank God who gave me every single thing I have. God gives us every tiny little thing in life and takes care of us all the time, even more than a mother can take care of her baby. We love our mothers, so we should love Allah. Don't you think so too, Grandma?'

I looked out over the valley with her, and what do you think I saw? You will never guess. I looked at the fields and the flowers, the birds and the insects, and in the distance all the things that humans had built and made and it was as if everything around me was speaking about the power and the beauty of Allah. I think my Grandma saw it too, because when I looked at her again and she turned towards me she was smiling.